Little Bl

Hope Digs a Hole

By Cecilia Minden

Hope wants to put up
a pole for vines.

Hope scopes out the yard.

"I will use a spade to dig a hole by this clover."

Hope starts to dig a hole and hits a big stone.

"I will put the pole by this slope."

Hope starts to dig a hole
and spots a little mole.

"I will put the pole closer to home."

Hope starts to dig a hole and spots a bone.

Ace drops the bone back in the hole.

Ace pushes dirt over the bone.

"I think I will plant the vines in a pot."

Hope plants the vines in a stone pot.

Word List

long a words	long i words	long o words	long u words
Ace	I	bone	use
spade	vines	closer	
		clover	
		hole	
		Hope	
		mole	
		pole	
		scopes	
		slope	
		stone	

106 Words

Hope wants to put up a pole for vines.
Hope scopes out the yard.
"I will use a spade to dig a hole by this clover."
Hope starts to dig a hole and hits a big stone.
"I will put the pole by this slope."
Hope starts to dig a hole and spots a little mole.
"I will put the pole closer to home."
Hope starts to dig a hole and spots a bone.
Ace drops the bone back in the hole.
Ace pushes dirt over the bone.
"I think I will plant the vines in a pot."
Hope plants the vines in a stone pot.

Published in the United States of America by Cherry Lake Publishing Group
Ann Arbor, Michigan
www.cherrylakepublishing.com

Illustrator: Tina Finn
Book Designer: Melinda Millward

Copyright © 2022 by Cherry Lake Publishing Group
All rights reserved. No part of this book may be reproduced or utilized in any form or by any means without written permission from the publisher.

Cherry Blossom Press is an imprint of Cherry Lake Publishing Group.

Library of Congress Cataloging-in-Publication Data

Names: Minden, Cecilia, author. | Finn, Tina, illustrator.
Title: Hope digs a hole / by Cecilia Minden ; illustrated by Tina Finn.
Description: Ann Arbor, Michigan : Cherry Lake Publishing, 2021. | Series: Little blossom stories | Audience: Grades K-1. | Summary: "Hope tries to find the perfect spot to plant her vines. This B-level story uses decodable text to raise confidence in early readers. The book features long o words, and uses a combination of sight words and long-vowel words in repetition to build recognition. Original illustrations help guide readers through the text"– Provided by publisher.
Identifiers: LCCN 2021024908 (print) | LCCN 2021024909 (ebook) | ISBN 9781534196858 (paperback) | ISBN 9781534197060 (pdf) | ISBN 9781534197275 (ebook)
Subjects: LCSH: Readers (Primary) | LCGFT: Readers (Publications) | Picture books.
Classification: LCC PE1119.2 .M563795 2021 (print) | LCC PE1119.2 (ebook) | DDC 428.6/2–dc23
LC record available at https://lccn.loc.gov/2021024908
LC ebook record available at https://lccn.loc.gov/2021024909

Cherry Lake Publishing Group would like to acknowledge the work of the Partnership for 21st Century Learning, a Network of Battelle for Kids. Please visit http://www.battelleforkids.org/networks/p21 for more information.

Printed in the United States of America
Corporate Graphics

Cecilia Minden is the former director of the Language and Literacy Program at Harvard Graduate School of Education. She earned her PhD in Reading Education at the University of Virginia. Dr. Minden has written extensively for early readers. She is passionate about matching children to the very book they need to improve their skills and progress to a deeper understanding of all the wonder books can hold. Dr. Minden and her family live in McKinney, Texas.